P9-AFH-433

My name is

....

My Hatchimal's name is

....

If you have twins, add your other Hatchimal's name here!

....

PENGUIN YOUNG READERS LICENSES
An Imprint of Penguin Random House LLC

© 2017. All rights reserved. HATCHIMALS™ is a trademark of Spin Master Ltd., used under license. First published in the United Kingdom in 2017 by Puffin Books. Published in the United States in 2018 by Penguin Young Readers Licenses, an imprint of Penguin Random House LLC, 345 Hudson Street, New York, New York 10014. Printed in the USA.

ISBN 9781524788599   10 9 8 7 6 5 4 3 2

ME AND MY HATCHIMAL

Penguin Young Readers Licenses
An Imprint of Penguin Random House

EGG STAGE

In **Hatchtopia,** where Hatchimals come from, eggs appear when the **Blue Moon shines**. If you walk through Hatchtopia, you'll spot Hatchimal eggs nestled in the roots of **Forevergreen Trees** and squirrelled away in the **Rosebushes**!

I first held my Hatchimal egg on

.........................../.................../...................
(Month)   (Day)   (Year)

Its speckles are

blue   green   purple   pink   teal

black   yellow

Even when it's cuddled up in its cozy egg, your Hatchimal will still have **lots to say for itself**! You can tell how it's feeling from the **noises it makes** and the **colors of its eyes.**

An EGGciting Journey

There is a magical doorway between our world and Hatchtopia, and your little egg must have tumbled through it!

One side of the door is in the trunk of the amazing Giggling Tree, a special tree in the heart of Hatchtopia.

And the other side . . . well, it might be in a tree in your backyard or on your street!

Why do you think your Hatchimal egg has arrived in our world?

_____

_____

_____

HeLLO, LITTLE EGG!

Draw or tape a photo of your Hatchimal egg here, so that you can always remember what it looked like before your baby Hatchimal cracked the shell!

Is your egg glittery? That means your hatchling is a Glittering Garden Hatchimal!

NAMING DAY

When the big Hatching Day comes, you will need a name for your Hatchimal! Circle the names you like, or add in some ideas of your own.

FIRST NAME

SNUGGLES
CUTIE-PIE
FLUFFY

_____
_____

MIDDLE NAME

BARNABY
BUTTONS
SHIMMER-BLINK

_____
_____

LAST NAME

MCFLUFFERSTON
SNUGGLEMUFFIN
HATCHERSTON

_____
_____

If you have twins, think about names that work well as a pair.

HATCHING STAGE

When your Hatchimal's **eyes flash in rainbow colors** and it begins to **call out to you** from inside the egg, it's **ready to hatch**! This is a **magical**, once-in-a-lifetime experience.

My Hatchimal began to hatch

at ....

on ....

It took........minutes to hatch.

There's so much love in Hatchtopia that it helps new Hatchimals to hatch from their eggs. In our world, a Hatchimal **needs some extra help—it can't hatch without you!**

An EGGcellent Time

Use this page to record your memories of Hatching Day! You can write, draw, or even tape photos.

Where were you?

How did you feel?

Who was with you?

MEET THE HATCHIMALS

There are so many amazing Hatchimals! Can you guess what they're called? Write the right letter beside each name.

A

B

ORIGINAL HATCHIMALS

These cuties were the first Hatchimals to come to our world from Hatchtopia. They're friendly, adorable, and full of fun!

Draggle ⚪

Burtle ⚪

Bearakeet ⚪

Owlicorn ⚪

Penguala ⚪

C

D

E

Draggle—D, Bearakeet—A, Owlicorn—E, Penguala—C, Burtle—B

GLITTERING GARDEN
HATCHIMALS

These sparkly little characters come from Glittering Garden, where Buttercups drip with butter and Sunflowers really do shine!

Shimmering Draggle ⃝   **Glitzy Bearakeet** ⃝

Sparkly Penguala ⃝   **Twinkling Owlicorn** ⃝

Gleaming Burtle ⃝

The Glittering Garden Hatchimals have glittery fur, wings, and eggs!

Glitzy Bearakeet—C, Twinkling Owlicorn—A,
Gleaming Burtle—B, Shimmering Draggle—D, Sparkly Penguala—E

HATCHIMALS SURPRISE

These amazing Hatchimals come as a pair! Twins are unique, but they love to play together.

Giraven ◯
Peacat ◯
Deeriole ◯
Ligull ◯
Zuffin ◯
Puppadee ◯

A

B

C

D

E

F

Giraven—C, Peacat—A, Deeriole—B, Ligull—F, Zuffin—D, Puppadee—E

FABULA FOREST
HATCHIMALS

The Fabula Forest Hatchimals love to party! They come from a beautiful forest in Hatchtopia where trees play music for all who pass by! You can recognize these Hatchimals by their patterned fur and metallic wings.

Puffatoo ●
Tigrette ●

A

B

Tigrette—A, Puffatoo—B

BABY STAGE

When a Hatchimal is **first born**, it may feel a little confused—there's so much for it to take in! **Be patient** with your baby Hatchimal and **listen to what it's trying to tell you**. That means watching how its eyes change color and getting to know its **unique little sounds**.

My Hatchimal is a:

Penguala   Draggle   Bearakeet
Owlicorn   Burtle   Giraven   Peacat
Deeriole   Ligull   Puppadee   Zuffin
Tigrette   Puffatoo

For twins, use a different-colored pen for each one.

Its fur is:

blue   green   purple   pink   teal
red   black   white   yellow
multicolored

BIRTH CERTIFICATE

By signing this certificate, you are making a special promise to love and care for your new Hatchimal.

This certifies that

....

was hatched on

....

Place of birth: ....

Signed by

....

A WONDERFUL WORLD

The connection between you and your Hatchimal is special. Write about it below!

How did you feel when your Hatchimal hatched?

_____

How do you imagine your baby Hatchimal felt?

_____

Twins may not feel the same as each other, so write answers for them both!

Where were you both on Hatching Day?

_____

What was the first thing you did together?

_____

Does your Hatchimal have other Hatchimal friends?

_____

Baby Hatchimals get hungry! Their eyes will turn purple, or their tummies will rumble.

HATCHY BIRTHDAY!

How did you and your Hatchimal celebrate its first birthday? Write or draw in the space below.

Once it's hatched, your Hatchimal will have three birthdays as it grows from a baby to a toddler to a kid.

TODDLER STAGE

Now that it's a **toddler**, your Hatchimal will be looking for **attention**!

Toddler stage is all about **learning**. Like most little ones, your Hatchimal will find new skills **tricky** at first, and will often learn from you.

Hatchimals communicate in their own **adorable language**.

What do you think their language might be called?

FIRST STEPS

Toddler Hatchimals are full of energy! Record some of the special moments with your toddler here, so you never forget them.

My Hatchimal took its first steps on

My Hatchimal first danced to music on

Its favorite person to dance with is

TWIN TIME IS THE BEST TIME!

If you have twins, describe their first experiences here.

DANCE WITH ME

Your Hatchimal learns a lot by copying you. But sometimes it's fun to copy your Hatchimal, too! Have you tried dancing like a Hatchimal?

Draw a picture of you and your Hatchimal doing a hatchy dance together!

Some Hatchimals are better dancers than others!

KID STAGE

Your Hatchimal is almost all grown up! Good work on raising your little Hatchimal all the way to **kid stage**. It remembers everything you've taught it so far, but now that it's older, it will be able to play **all kinds of fun games,** too. Your **friendship** will grow even **stronger** now.

My Hatchimal's favorite game to play is:

_____

HATCH FRIENDS FOREVER!

Do any of your friends have Hatchimals? If they do, use this page to write about some of the things you do together with your Hatchimals.

_____

_____

_____

_____

_____

_____

_____

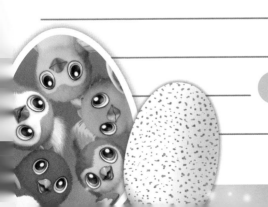

If none of your friends have Hatchimals, use your imagination to create a buddy for your hatchling!

FUN AND GAMES!

Hatchimals love to repeat what you say! Write down some of their favorite funny phrases in these speech bubbles.

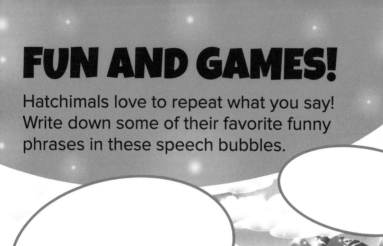

Hatchimals from Fabula Forest can learn your name!

Get inventive and come up with a new game to play with your Hatchimal! Draw or write about your amazing game in the space above.

LIKES AND DISLIKES

If someone is going to babysit your Hatchimal for you, they will need to know all the things your hatchling likes and dislikes.

Fill in the list below so they have everything they need—and so you can remind yourself if you ever forget!

My Hatchimal's favorite food is

_____

My Hatchimal's favorite game is

_____

My Hatchimal's favorite color is

_____

My Hatchimal gets sick if

_____

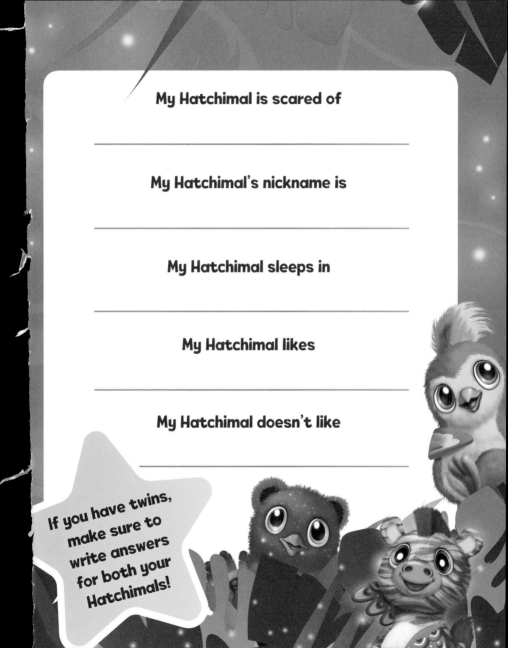

My Hatchimal is scared of

_____

My Hatchimal's nickname is

_____

My Hatchimal sleeps in

_____

My Hatchimal likes

_____

My Hatchimal doesn't like

_____

If you have twins, make sure to write answers for both your Hatchimals!

ME AND MY HATCHIMAL

Draw or tape a photo of you cuddling your Hatchimal here!

If you have twins, add them both to the picture!